The Incredible Adventures of Daniel:

A Strong Young Man with Great Faith

Luisette Kraal

Chapter 1
The Soldiers Arrived

Daniel walked through the city of Jerusalem, passing by a colorful market where sellers offered their goods, and the air was filled with the aroma of spices.

"Good morning, Mr. Eli!" Daniel greeted an old man who was selling fruit.

Mr. Eli smiled and handed him a fresh apple. "Take it, young man, so you'll have energy."

"Thank you! Today is a good day," Daniel said as he took a bite of the apple.

"This is what your mother needs for cooking," Mr. Eli added, giving Daniel a wooden box filled with spices, vegetables, and eggs.

"Thank you, Mr. Eli," Daniel replied. "I'll take it quickly because my mom needs to finish preparing the food for tomorrow—it's temple day," he explained.

A Big Change

Far away, in the old city of Babylon, there was a king named Nebuchadnezzar.

Ne-bu-chad-nez-zar

He was a powerful and feared king. His soldiers were strong. Their armor shone under the sun, and their swords made loud noises as they moved. One day, King Nebuchadnezzar's army marched toward Jerusalem, and their footsteps echoed through the streets. News of their arrival spread quickly, and the people of Judah felt very scared.

As the soldiers drew closer, the ground beneath Daniel and his friends started to shake. Families hugged each other and looked out their windows with fear. Some hid; others fell to the ground and wept. A group of people, however, kept their faith and began to pray.

A few days later, the army seized the city, rushing toward the temple—a holy place everyone loved. They broke down the doors and stole golden cups and treasures. That day was chaotic and sad. Many families tried to hide, but the soldiers didn't just steal—they also took people as prisoners.

That is how Daniel and his friends were forced to walk back to Babylon with the soldiers. That is how they became captives.

As they walked, Daniel closed his eyes and prayed to God. So did his friends.

"We can't give up!" Daniel encouraged his friends Hananiah, Mishael, and Azariah, who were also very scared.

"Our dad is probably praying for us in the temple," Daniel said. They all missed their temple and their families, but they knew their lives had changed.

"Don't worry, guys!" Daniel said with a calming smile. "Even if our parents aren't here, we can still pray together and trust that God is with us."

His words gave them hope, and the four friends believed that God would not leave them in this new land.

A New Home

When they arrived in Babylon, king Nebuchadnezzar ordered that the smartest and strongest young men serve him and his court. He called Ashpenaz, the head

of his officials, and said, "Find me strong and handsome boys from Israel. I want smart boys who learn quickly and can serve in my palace."

He had a clear idea of the kind of boys he wanted—no physical problems, full of wisdom, and eager to be taught. They would need to learn Babylonian customs, language, and read books.

Ashpenaz set out to find the perfect boys.

Among those chosen were Daniel, Hananiah, Mishael, and Azariah. When they entered the palace for the first time, they were amazed by the beautiful decorations and the smell of fancy food in the air.

The king told them what to eat, but the food was very rich and greasy. The boys weren't sure if God would want them to eat that feast. Also, the king drank a lot of wine—something their families didn't permit.

So Daniel said to his friends, "Let's ask Ashpenaz if we can eat only vegetables and drink water."

The young men liked the idea and approached the official. He was worried—they might become weak or sick, and the king might be upset. But, in the end,

Ashpenaz agreed.

So, for ten days, the boys ate only vegetables and drank water as a test.

Test of Faith

As the days went by, Daniel and his friends focused on their studies while enjoying their simple meals.

They helped each other, built their friendships, shared dreams, studied, and prayed together. Despite the difficulties with language and customs, they were determined to do well.

After ten days, Ashpenaz checked their health and was surprised—these four friends looked healthier and stronger than the others who had eaten the king's rich food.

"From now on, you can keep eating only vegetables and drinking water," Ashpenaz said, impressed.

However, he didn't like their original names and gave them new Babylonian names:

- Daniel became Belteshazzar

- Hananiah became Shadrach

- Mishael became Meshach

- Azariah became Abednego

Even with their new names, they remained faithful to God and kept their trust in Him. God blessed Daniel and his friends because of their dedication. Ashpenaz also observed that they could understand complex books and solve math problems easily.

Three years later, the king called all the young men to him for a test.

Daniel and his friends were nervous— "What will the king say to us?" they wondered. But everything went smoothly.

King Nebuchadnezzar was amazed by their wisdom. He asked them many questions, and they answered ten times better than the other young men. No one was as intelligent as they were, so the king chose them to serve in his palace.

Daniel told his friends, "I know you miss your families, but let's show the king that we are faithful servants of our God. We will continue following what our parents taught us and trust in the Lord."

Chapter 2

The New Life

One night, the king of Babylon couldn't sleep. He had a strange dream that made him feel worried and scared. He woke up feeling confused and desperately wanted to understand what the nightmare meant.

Immediately, he called all his wise men, magicians, and helpers to meet him in the palace.

"I need you to tell me what I dreamed and what it means!" he commanded.

The wise men were unsure and nervous. They asked, "Please tell us the dream, and we will explain it to you."

But king Nebuchadnezzar responded, "No. I want you to tell me what I dreamed. If you don't, I won't believe that you understand anything."

The men cried out, "No one can tell you your dream—that's impossible!"

The king grew very angry and warned them that if they failed, they would be punished. The men trembled with fear because they knew their lives depended on solving the mystery.

The Prayer

When Daniel heard what was happening, he wanted to help. He went to the king's guard, Arioch, and said, "Please give me a little time so I can ask my God for the answer."

Arioch agreed, glad someone was willing to try to solve the mystery.

Later, Daniel returned to his friends—Shadrach, Meshach, and Abednego.

"We need to pray! God can show us the king's dream," he said.

They held hands and prayed, asking God for wisdom and understanding.

That same night, God answered their prayers and revealed the meaning of the dream to Daniel in a vision.

Full of gratitude, Daniel hurried to see king Nebuchadnezzar.

"Your Majesty," Daniel began, "I know what your dream means. No wise man, magician, or helper can explain it. But I can tell you because my God has shown it to me. The God of Heaven, who knows all secrets, has revealed it. That's why I can explain it to you. God is showing you, king Nebuchadnezzar, what will happen in the future."

The Dream

"You had a dream about a great statue," Daniel said confidently.

The king listened carefully as Daniel described the amazing statue: Its head was made of gold, its chest and arms of silver, its belly and thighs of bronze, its legs of iron, and its feet a mixture of iron and clay.

Daniel continued, "As you watched, a rock was cut out—but not by human hands. It struck the statue and crushed it. The iron, clay, bronze, silver, and gold all broke into pieces and turned to dust. The wind carried them away so nothing was left. But the rock grew into a huge mountain that filled the entire earth."

"Exactly!" the king shouted. "That's my dream!"

Daniel explained, "The statue represents different kingdoms. You, king, are the head of gold. After you, other kingdoms will rise. In the end, the statue will be destroyed, and the true king will come to reign over the world. He is the ROCK, and His kingdom will last forever!"

The Rock

King Nebuchadnezzar was amazed. He saw how powerful Daniel's God was, and he bowed down to praise Him.

He said, "Your God is the God of gods and the King of kings. He doesn't need a statue—he can even use a rock!"

The king gave Daniel an important role in the kingdom, appointing him in charge of many important places.

Daniel returned to his friends with a big smile.

"We did it together! Our prayers were answered!" he told Shadrach, Meshach, and Abednego, who smiled back. They stayed faithful and supported each other through the whole challenge.

From this adventure, Daniel learned that with faith, prayer, and a little courage, amazing things can happen—even in a big city far from home. As he continued to serve in the palace, he knew that God was always with him, guiding him every step of the way.

Chapter 3
The Trumpets Sound

King Nebuchadnezzar ruled over the vast kingdom of Babylon, and he wanted everyone to honor him. One day, he made a huge golden statue that shone brightly in the sun. Then he gave an order: "Every time you hear the music—trumpets, flutes, zithers, harps, lyres, pipes, and other instruments—you must bow down and worship this statue!"

The people of Babylon were afraid of the king, so whenever the music played, they all bowed to the

statue — even those who didn't truly want to.

At that time, Daniel wasn't in the city.

But his three brave friends—Shadrach, Meshach, and Abednego—loved God very much. When they heard the king's command, they looked at each other. They knew what God wanted them to do: follow the true, living God, and worship only Him.

Then the trumpets sounded.

But they didn't move.

They stood still and did not bow.

Standing Tall

Some of the king's jealous officials noticed that Shadrach, Meshach, and Abednego were standing while everyone else was kneeling. They ran to tell King Nebuchadnezzar.

"Your Majesty," they said, "those three young men you brought from Jerusalem aren't obeying your order! They refuse to worship your statue!"

The king was furious. He summoned Shadrach, Meshach, and Abednego to come to him.

"Is it true you won't bow down to the statue I made?" he asked angrily.

Without fear, the three friends answered, "We will serve the king in every way we can, but we cannot worship any god except our God."

"You won't worship my statue?!" the king shouted, his face turning red with anger.

"Next time, when you hear the music, you better bow down and worship the statue. If you don't, I will throw you into a blazing furnace! Then, what god could possibly save you from my hand?"

The Blazing Furnace

"We don't need to defend ourselves to you," they replied. "Our God can save us from the fire. But even if He doesn't, we still won't worship your statue!"

The king was even more furious. He ordered the

furnace to be heated seven times hotter than usual. His strongest guards tied up Shadrach, Meshach, and Abednego and threw them into the flames. The fire was so hot that the soldiers near it were burned up!

But then something amazing happened. As the king watched the fire, he saw four people walking inside the flames—not just three.

"Didn't we throw three men into the fire?" the king asked.

"Why do I see four? And the fourth looks like a god!"

Unharmed

The king ran to the edge of the furnace and shouted, "Shadrach, Meshach, Abednego—servants of the Most High God—come out!"

The three friends walked out of the fire, and to everyone's surprise, they weren't hurt at all! Their clothes weren't burned, and they didn't even smell like smoke!

King Nebuchadnezzar was amazed. He praised God and said, "There is no other god who can save like this!" He saw that the God of Shadrach, Meshach, and Abednego was powerful and worthy of worship.

From that day on, the king made a new law: "no one in Babylon was allowed to speak against their God."

God hadn't just saved their lives—He had used their faith to show everyone how great He was.

So, the three brave friends kept serving God faithfully, knowing that He was always with them—even in a fiery furnace.

They had learned that standing strong in their faith could bring amazing miracles.

Chapter 4
No Other God

One night, king Nebuchadnezzar had another strange dream that made him feel uneasy.

He saw a huge tree reaching up to the sky. It was so big that animals rested under its shade, and birds lived in its branches.

But suddenly, a voice from heaven shouted, "Cut down the tree! Leave only the stump!"

The king woke up afraid.

"I need to know what this dream means!" he said.

He called all his wise men, magicians, and fortune tellers, but none of them could explain it.

Frustrated, the king shouted, "No one can help me!

Where is Daniel? He can tell me the meaning!"

At once, one of the king's helpers said, "Call for Daniel!"

When Daniel arrived, the king explained the dream and asked for help. Daniel prayed to God, and God showed him the meaning.

With courage, Daniel said, "The tree in your dream, O king, represents you. You have become very powerful, but your pride will bring you down. If you become humble and recognize God, your kingdom will be given back to you."

The Warning Ignored

The king listened to Daniel's warning. He was troubled, but he didn't change his ways.

"Me? Fall? Never!" he thought proudly.

Sometime later, as the king was walking in his palace, he said, "Look at this great city of Babylon! I built it with my own power!"

Right then, a voice from heaven said, "King Nebuchadnezzar, your kingdom is taken away!"

Suddenly, the king lost his mind. He started living like a wild animal—eating grass and sleeping outside in the fields. He stayed like this for seven years.

But one day, he looked up to the sky, and his mind became clear again. He finally understood that God is the true ruler over everything.

Then, he began to praise God and said:

"His kingdom lasts forever.

He rules over everything.

God does what He knows is right.

And now I praise Him for His justice."

The King Returns

After this, King Nebuchadnezzar went back to his palace. God restored his kingdom to him—this time, even more powerful than before. But this time, the king was humble. He taught the people to respect and honor God.

"It is always important to stay humble," the king told his subjects. "Because God can bring down those who are proud."

Daniel smiled when he saw how much the king had changed. Now, the king told everyone about God's love. His story became a lesson for the entire kingdom.

Children and adults listened in amazement. Daniel and his friends continued to teach that trusting God brings hope, even in the darkest times.

Chapter 5

King's Party

Some time later, King Nebuchadnezzar's son, Belshazzar, became king. He loved throwing parties. One day, he invited a thousand guests—nobles, friends, and important officials. The palace was filled with music, laughter, and dancing.

The king sat on his throne, surrounded by elaborate food and golden cups filled with wine.

"Dance! Celebrate!" he shouted joyfully. "Let's enjoy how great my kingdom is!"

Everyone drank and partied until they were all drunk.

Then, Belshazzar had a terrible idea.

"Bring me the golden and silver cups we brought from the temple in Jerusalem!" he ordered. "We will use them to toast to our gods!"

A Mysterious Message

The servants were afraid. Those cups were holy—they had been taken from God's temple. The servants didn't want to use them for a wild party, but they had no choice but to obey the king.

The king and his nobles drank from the sacred cups, laughing and praising false gods made of gold and silver.

Suddenly, something incredible happened.

A hand appeared out of nowhere and began writing on the palace wall!

Everyone froze.

"What is that?" shouted a noble, trembling with fear.

"A...a...hand..." said another with a white face. "Just one hand...no body to it....just the hand."

The king turned pale, and his legs shook. "It is writing on the wall! What does it say? Who can read it?" he cried.

Calling Daniel

No one at the party could understand the strange writing on the wall.

It said:

MENE

MENE

TEKEL

PARSIN

The king quickly summoned his magicians and wise men, but none could interpret the message.

"I will give a purple robe and a gold chain to anyone who can tell me what it means!" the king promised.

Just then, the queen entered.

"Long live the king!" she said. She remembered Daniel. "Don't be afraid king. Call for Daniel—he can solve this mystery."

When Daniel arrived, the king said,

"Are you Daniel, the one from Judah? I need your help. If you tell me what the writing means, I will give you great gifts."

Daniel replied, "I don't want your gifts. But I will tell you what the writing means."

He looked at the words on the wall and then reminded the king of his father, King Nebuchadnezzar, who learned the hard way that pride and dishonouring God are dangerous.

Daniel's Message

"Your Majesty," Daniel began, "you have not honored the true God. You used His special cups for a party and praised false gods. Here's what the words mean:

MENE- God has numbered the days of your Kingdom, and it is almost over.

TEKEL- You have been weighed and found wanting.

PARSIN- Your kingdom will be divided and given to the Medes and Persians."

The king listened carefully, trembling. Deep inside, he knew Daniel was telling the truth.

Even though the news was bad, he thanked Daniel and kept his promise—he dressed him in fine clothes and made him the third highest ruler in the kingdom.

But the king soon realized that this wouldn't save him.

The Fall of the King

That very night, the Medes and Persians invaded Babylon. Just as Daniel had predicted, King Belshazzar's kingdom came to an end.

From that moment on, everyone remembered the message written on the wall: Disrespecting God leads to serious consequences.

The king had lost everything because of his pride.

As everything around him fell apart, Belshazzar whispered,

"Daniel... you were right. I should have listened to God."

A new king took the throne. His name was Darius.

Chapter 6

The New Law

King Darius continued to rule, and he quickly noticed that Daniel was wise and faithful. The king liked him very much and decided to make him one of the highest officials in the kingdom.

But the other officials grew jealous.

"We can't let this guy from Jerusalem be more powerful than us!" they whispered among themselves.

So, they devised a plan to get rid of him.

"Let's make a law that says no one can pray to any god or person—except the king—for 30 days," they said with evil smiles.

King Darius didn't realize it was a trap, and he signed the new law.

When Daniel heard about it, he faced two choices:

- Stop praying to God, or

- Follow his heart and remain faithful.

Daniel's Decision

That evening, Daniel went home, opened his windows facing Jerusalem—just as he always did—and began to pray.

"Lord, You are my shelter," he whispered. "I can't stop talking to You."

His friends, Shadrach, Meshach, and Abednego, came to visit and prayed too.

"Daniel, have you heard about the new law?" they asked anxiously. "We are in danger!"

Daniel smiled calmly. "I can't stop praying," he said. "God has always been with me, and I will continue trusting Him."

The Lions' Den

The next day, the officials saw Daniel praying.

"We caught him!" they shouted triumphantly.

They brought Daniel before King Darius.

"Your friend Daniel has broken the law!" they told him.

The king was very sad because he cared for Daniel.
But he knew the law could not be changed.

"I can't do anything," Darius said reluctantly. "Daniel, you must be thrown into the lions' den."

With a heavy heart, the king added, "May your God, whom you serve faithfully, rescue you."

Daniel was taken to the den. Inside, lions growled and roared — but Daniel felt peace.

"God, I know You are with me," he said as he entered.

The lions came near, but they didn't attack.

God sent His angel to shut the lions' mouths.

That night, King Darius couldn't sleep. He was worried about Daniel.

At sunrise, he hurried to the lions' den and cried out,

"Daniel! Are you okay?"

And Daniel replied calmly,

"I'm here, Your Majesty!"

Daniel's Victory

Darius was amazed. "You made it out of the lions' den!" he exclaimed.

Daniel smiled. "My God protected me. He heard my prayers."

The king was so grateful that he issued a new law: "Everyone must respect the God of Daniel! He is the One who saves and rescues!"

From that day forward, Daniel was safe, and he was also able to share his faith openly with the whole city.

An Example of Faith

The story of Daniel in the lions' den teaches us that faith in God gives us courage, even in fearful moments.

Daniel was brave, and his trust in God brought blessings to all of Babylon.

From that day on, Daniel continued serving the king and sharing with others how great his God is.

We all need faith, prayer, and courage!

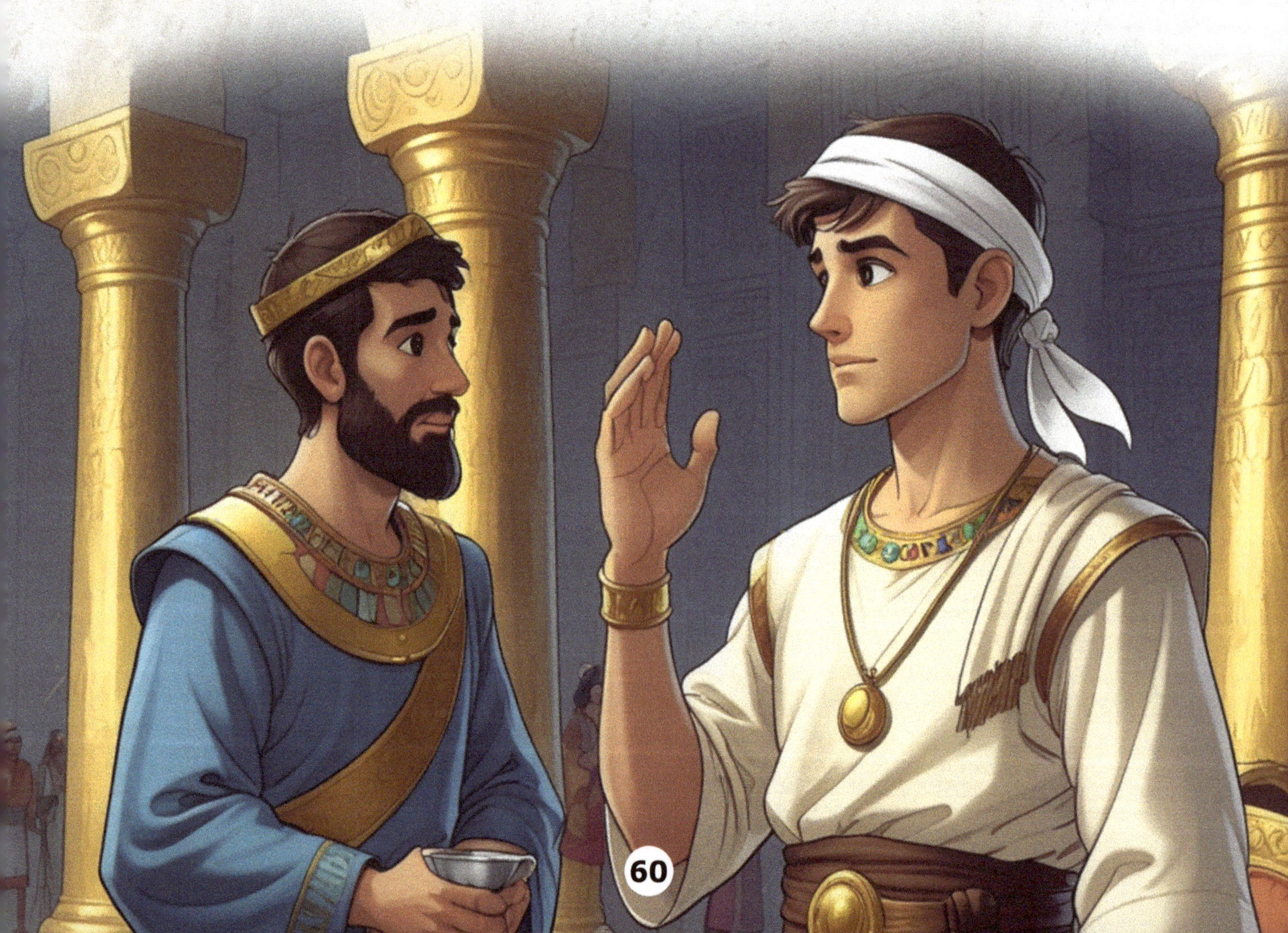

List of Bible verses mentioning the word "ROCK":

1. Deuteronomy 32:4: "He is the Rock, his works are perfect, and all his ways are just. God is faithful; he does no wrong. He is righteous and just" (NIV).

2. 2 Samuel 22:32: "For who is God besides the Lord? And who is the Rock except our God?" (NIV).

3. Psalm 18:2: "The Lord is my rock, my fortress and my deliverer; my God is my rock, in whom I take refuge. He is my shield and the horn of my salvation, my stronghold!" (NIV).

4. Psalm 31:3: "Since you are my rock and my fortress, for the sake of your name lead and guide me" (NIV).

5. Psalm 62:6: "He alone is my rock and my salvation; he is my fortress, I will not be shaken" (NIV).

6. Isaiah 26:4: "Trust in the Lord forever, for the Lord, the Lord himself, is the Rock eternal" (NIV).

7. Matthew 7:24: "Therefore everyone who hears these words of mine and puts them into practice is like a wise man who built his house on the rock" (NIV).

8. 1 Corinthians 10:4: "They drank from the spiritual rock that accompanied them, and that rock was Christ" (NIV).